THE VOICE OF
BUGLE ANN

BOOKS BY
MacKINLAY KANTOR

———

THE VOICE

of

BUGLE ANN

By MacKINLAY KANTOR

F
K

COWARD-McCANN, INC.

New York

6402

To
Dennis M. Kelly

NOTE.

All thanks to George Proctor, Will Martindale, Dan Longwell and Tom Duncan; and to certain fox-hounds of high and noble birth. THE AUTHOR

1

HER VOICE was something to dream about, on any night when she was running through the hills. The first moment she was old enough to boast an individual voice, Springfield Davis swore that she would be a great dog, and within another month he had given her the name she carried so proudly.

One of her great-grandfathers, many generations removed, had followed Spring Davis away from home when he went off to join General Claiborne Jackson and his homespun army among the prickly-orange hedges, so there was logic in the inheritance which put that trumpet in her throat.

She was slender, like hounds of the Spaulding line, and not as sprawling or cumbersome as the good-natured, long-tongued Walkers.

Any one in Missouri who knew anything about fox-hounds had heard of the Davis dogs, but somehow there never came to be a Davis line. It was all in the family, and there existed a haughtiness in the old man which wouldn't permit him to have Davis dogs running anywhere except in the ranges along Heaven Creek. That was why Bugle Ann was still a maiden at five years, long after old Calhoun Royster or the Lanceys would have seen to it that she carried on her business in life.

And Spring Davis was prudish past the point of ridicule, though no one would have dared to laugh at him. He hated the common word for a female dog, and would not let it touch his tongue. He called his she-dogs ladies or girls, and there was a firm beauty about him when he spoke to them. You wouldn't think that a man like that could ever be tried for murder, or become a convict.

Those things did happen to Spring Davis, at eighty-two. They didn't affect him as they would have affected most men of eighty-two. Whenever he heard the gongs and whistles which sent him about his gray routine at Jefferson City, he must have banished those sounds from his consciousness. He must have imagined instead that he was sitting by a fire at the edge of Bachelor's timber, listening to the dogs as they hunted out of Chilly Branch Hollow, with Bugle Ann's cry echoing against the blackness of the sky.

2

"BAKE," SAID old Cal Royster, "put some wood on."

Baker went to the woodpile beyond the red circle and found a piece of rotten stump. "We'll have a good moon by next week," he said, and jammed the wood upon the coals.

"I don't give shucks for moonlight," exclaimed Cal Royster. "Give me a black-dark night, when the fox ain't shadow-shy. Any fool ought to know that. I don't know where my boys get such notions as moonlight nights."

Across the fire, Spring Davis tapped his pipe against the heel of his boot. He stopped, suddenly, head tilted to one side. The firelight turned his shaggy mustache and eyebrows to fluid metal.

"Listen," he said. "Getting sweet."

His son, Benjy Davis, rose to his feet. He moved like an Indian; so did his father. There was something of the Indian in Benjy's twenty-year-old face, tanned and narrow and bony.

His black eyes glittered. "He's a mighty sweet fox if they've had him away over toward the river! We ain't heard a sound for twenty minutes."

There were five men around that fire at the edge of Bachelor's timber. Four of them— Spring Davis and his only son, Benjy, and Calhoun Royster and his oldest son, Baker— were the most ardent fox-hound men in the county. The fifth man was no hound man at all; he was a new insurance agent from Wolf Center. He had eaten supper at the Davises', and he was beside that fire only by invitation and sufferance.

He inquired, "What do you mean, Mr. Davis? 'Getting sweet.'"

"It sweats," Spring told him. "The fox does. They can smell him better after he's been running awhile. That's 'getting sweet.' "

Now even the agent's untrained ears could detect a faint distraction amid the common night sounds—the hush of sleeping forests that never sleep, and which is really no hush at all. The sound came from over past the Armstrong place, far past Chilly Branch and across the ridge beyond, and it was as eerie and elusive as the calling of wild geese.

"You'll hear her in a minute," whispered Springfield Davis.

The confused murmur became a tiny baying: the tongues of many dogs, eager and striving in spite of their two-hour run.

"That's Toul Sector," Bake Royster declared. Bake had been in the war, and all the Royster dogs were named Toul Sector or Border Service or General Bullard or some such name.

"It's not Toul Sector," said Benjy. "Not that nearest one."

Calhoun Royster's tone showed the jealous annoyance which he displayed frequently with the self-assured Davises. "It's no Bugle Ann, neither," he snorted. "Nor no Bill Bryan, nor Cox, nor Frances Cleveland, nor any Davis dog."

"Reckon it is a bit turkey-mouthed for one of ours."

Old Spring Davis loved to hear Cal swear in his beard. So he continued, "I'll tell you, Cal. It's an Armstrong dog. They've picked up an Armstrong as they come past."

Royster stood with head wiggling on his humped shoulders, his bearded lips hanging open as he tried to take that baying apart and examine it.

"What Armstrong dog?" he demanded. He seemed to be weakening.

"I'd say it was Jackie Cooper, that little pale-faced two-year-old."

Old man Royster listened a moment longer. He gave a defeated snort. Then his ire mounted. "Where in hell's Bugle Ann, anyway?"

"Maybe she'll quit, and come in," muttered his son.

Benjy whirled, and for a moment the insurance agent thought that he was going to strike Bake Royster. "No Davis dog ever come in without being called, before a fox holed," Benjy said. "Except one. You remember him. We shot him the next day."

Spring nodded. "Easy boy.... Guess there's bound to be a black sheep in every tribe, though this dog was white. Don't you folks worry about Bugle Ann. You'll hear her soon enough."

"Pshaw, scat," said Bake, uneasily, "I was just joking."

On such a night as this, with clouds covering the stars and no southeast wind smothering the scent, you could tell that the hounds were running with their heads high. They skirted the eastern boundary of Chilly Branch Hollow, and straightened out along the higher ridge which swung toward Bachelor's woods.

All the men were on their feet.

"You talk moonlight," Royster chided his son. "Never get a fox to keep the high ground except on this kind of night. Lose half the sound when them dogs get in a gulley."

There was a turkey-mouth among those ringing voices; old Spring had been right about the Armstrong dog. The Royster dogs were mainly chop-mouthed, and they sent their clipped, bristling bay like a volley across the wooded plateau.

"I don't hear her, Pa," whispered Benjy Davis, with some concern.

The old man held up his hand. Suddenly a new cry was born amid all the hissing of excited crickets.

For some reason, the Wolf Center insur-

ance agent felt the hair prickle on his neck.
... This was no hound-voice such as he had
ever heard before, and he would never hear its
like again. It was a bugle—the Davises had a
rare poetry in their make-up, thought young
Mr. Mayor of the National Emblem Liability. He stood there with his nails cutting his
palms, and listened.

"That's her, all right," came Cal Royster's
admission, "but why's she kiting off by herself? If she hain't lost it, I'm loony."

Spring Davis repeated the word, "Lost,"
and smiled into the fire. . . . There had never
been a sound like that in the Heaven Creek
country until Bugle Ann was born; even now
the trumpet-cry knew its own pride, and
swung off toward the southeast, far ahead of
the *owk-owk-owk-owk* with which the Royster
dogs threatened.

The old man whooped, without any warning: "Now, there they go after her!"

Left, around the last spur of Bachelor's

woods, the welter of hounds went sweeping after Bugle Ann. Her cry soared ahead—high, round, with that queer and brassy resonance which made you think that ghosts were out there somewhere, sounding Taps without any armies to follow them.

Springfield Davis came back to the fire and squatted on his heels. "You see," he told the insurance agent, "Bugle Ann was running that same fox night-before-last. I reckon she remembered how he likes to feint west along a little draw that's over there, and then double back and cut his own trail. It's a common fox trick if the fox has got the nerve to try it, and easy for him to work when the scent's heavy."

"I'm afraid," said Mr. Mayor, "that I don't understand."

"Well," said Cal Royster, somewhat reluctantly, "the average dog is bound to foller the way he's headed, if the smell is hauling him."

They were silent for a moment, listening to the baying as it swam fainter and fainter into the darkness.

"I'm afraid I don't understand any of this," Mr. Mayor cried with honesty. "I came from the East, just this year. They gave me this Missouri territory and— Fox-hunting! If you hunt every night or two, I don't see how you have any foxes left."

Bake Royster added more wood to the fire, and Benjy Davis brought up the sandwich sack. "We never kill the fox," said Spring, sharply. "We don't ride no horses, nor wear funny coats and caps. We raise dogs, and train them."

Waken, lords and ladies gay, thought Mr. Mayor in his baffled mind. *All the jolly chase is here, with*... "But it's really just a race between fox and dogs, then?"

"Fox holes up when he gets tired, and the dogs come home."

"And the same fox will run again, another night?"

"There's quite a slew of them around. Plenty of mice and ground-squirrels for them to eat; they never bother no hen roosts. Yes, they run again. Night after night, and year after year."

Benjy opened a battered vacuum bottle and poured a cup of coffee for his father. The gray-headed man touched the hot tin cup with cautious fingers. "Year after year," he repeated, dreamily.

The insurance agent choked over a bacon sandwich. "Are you folks—and you also, Mr. Royster—the only people who do this sort of thing?"

Spring Davis looked up from the fire. "Young man, did you ever hear of Old Man Spaulding? Reckon not. Or Gentry German, Parrish, or Colonel Trigg?"

"I suppose," Mr. Mayor replied, "that those are dogs."

"Those are men who made fox-hound history in America. And Wash Maupin, and **Robert Rodes, and James Kanatzar.** You see, sir, it's a matter of breeding good dogs—and understanding them—and—kind of loving them. It—" He broke off suddenly.

Cal Royster blinked at the gems of flame which shone through the whisky flask in his hand. "Speaking of names, Spring," he began, "you ought to take our friend here, over to the Armstrongs. You see, mister, Ed Armstrong is mighty religious and his boys are mighty the other way."

"Always going to town," put in Bake, "to dances and moving pictures and rotation pool, and things."

His father insisted, "But they do hunt. They name their dogs after moving picture actors. Old Ed Armstrong, he names his after religious folks. Until you've heard the Armstrong pack after a good, sweet fox, you hain't heard a thing. All turkey-mouthed, or squawl-horn-chop-mouthed at the best. Until you've heard Billy Sunday and Jackie Cooper and Dwight L. Moody and Zasu Pitts and Hoot Gibson and Mary Magdalene all driving a fox at once, you never have had no treat give to you."

"They're good bench dogs," said Spring Davis. He didn't like to hear too much laughter directed at the Armstrongs. "They mostly got stylish tails and compact feet and good stifles. If you like bench, the Armstrong dogs just hustle in the points."

He held up his hand, and Cal Royster put away the whisky bottle.

"Coming in," Davis prophesied. "I can get it, from 'way south, at the top of Heaven Creek."

Benjy swore; his face was very dark. "Blame fox won't give them more'n three hours any more."

"That's a fact," nodded his father. "We'll

have to try farther up Heaven Creek to-morrow."

Mr. Mayor burst out, "Good Lord, do you
do this all night, every night? When do you
do your farm work?" He began to understand why Spring Davis had been unable to
renew his fire insurance policy.

"Not every night," said Springfield.
"Sometimes it rains. Or just the opposite,
sometimes the weather's been too dry. Or we
get long damp spells—too damp—or we get
low southeast winds. We don't come out every
night."

"Mr. Davis," cried Mr. Mayor of the National Emblem Liability, "how old are you?"

Spring smiled into the fire. "Seventy years
ago this season, I ran off to join the Confed-
erate army. I was only twelve, but I had done
a sight of fox-hunting before that."

The hounds came closer, and once more
Bugle Ann's blare was riding high above
their hooted chorus.

"He's striking for his hole," Bake said. "In a minute he'll hand them the raspberry."

Spring Davis leaned back and closed his eyes. He drew a deep breath. "Waited seventy years to have a dog like that," he whispered to nobody in particular.

The fox uttered his shout of defiance—that strange yelp which was half a cat-cry, half a dog-bark, and wholly insulting. Then baffled shrieks told that he had holed.

"Fetch the horn, Benjy," ordered old Davis. "I don't want her sporting around."

Cal Royster bristled. "This ain't August nor yet February. You talk like our dogs was a pack of hoodlums."

"I just like to have her to home, Cal."

From beside a rolled up sweater, Benjy Davis brought a battered army bugle and gave it to his father. The old man wet his lips, fitted the mouthpiece carefully beneath his shaggy mustache, and blew two notes: the *ta-da* of galloping Valkyries, forever a summons and a challenge.

"Will she come for that?" Mr. Mayor asked in amazement.

"Always."

Benjy peered toward the crossing at Heaven Creek. "Looks like some other folks are coming, too."

The dull, yellow lights of an old Ford were rocking toward them, and they could hear the chatter of its motor. "That'll be Tom and Delbert, I reckon," said Cal Royster. "Don't know what's got into them. Been to see the Lancey girls again. They'd ruther spark around with two flibberty-gibbets than be out with the dogs."

Slowly the Ford rattled up the hill, and stopped at the wood road. The two younger Royster boys got out with cheers of greeting, which were stilled hastily when they saw a stranger at the fire.

"How's the calf market?" taunted their elder brother.

"Never you mind," grunted Delbert Royster. He and Tom were sunburned, strapping youngsters who would have looked happier in overalls than in the Sunday suits they had worn for their squiring.

Their faces were unwontedly serious, and neither of them headed for the sandwiches.

"What in time ails you two?" demanded Cal.

"You heard about the old Camden place?" countered Delbert.

Every one except the insurance agent looked automatically toward the northwest. A mile down the valley of Heaven Creek stood an abandoned house and farm buildings, which in daylight showed plainly from their hill.

"I did hear that somebody was moving on it," said the father.

"Some of the Camdens, coming back," added Baker.

Old Spring Davis stood fingering his bugle. "The Camdens was great dog people in their day. That's twenty-thirty year ago."

"Well," said Tom, "we heard about it over at Lancey's. It's a son-in-law of the old Camdens, and his name is Terry, and he aims to raise sheep."

For a long moment no one spoke.

"Fence," said Spring Davis. There was an odd whine in his tone.

Delbert brought out a sack of Bull Durham, and began to make a cigarette. "Martin Lancey was at the lumberyard to-day, and this Terry was there. He was ordering posts and wire. Wove-wire, Lancey said."

"Hog-tight, bull-strong and horse-high," added Tom.

A coal popped in the fire, and a shower of sparks blew up.

Spring Davis said, thoughtfully: "Man's name is Jacob Terry. I remember him."

"Sure enough," agreed Calhoun Royster, "and he married Effie Camden. I heard she died, up in Jackson County. Had one daughter, seems to me."

Spring Davis put down the bugle. His knee-joints creaked as he stood up. "I wouldn't call this Jake Terry a pleasant man. Once he whipped a horse with a piece of board . . . going to put up a wove-wire fence, hey?"

"They're moving in, this week," went on Delbert. "Mrs. Lancey said there was a light in the house early to-night."

Something twitched outside the last reaches of firelight, and Spring Davis went down on one knee. "Come on, little lady," he cried. Bugle Ann trotted into the light, her long ears flapping, her elbows plastered with mud. She was a small hound, but with a strong, well-arched coupling, and she carried her tail like a banner.

Davis took her in his arms. "This here's the angel song you heard, Mr. Mayor."

"She didn't come very prompt," scoffed old Royster.

"Prompt enough," said the veteran. "She set out there past the light, until she was sure about that car. You didn't know the Royster boys would come driving up in their smoke-wagon, did you, honey?"

She wiped his chin with her limp tongue.

"What do you feed her?" asked Mr. Mayor.

"Best cornmeal, bran, and pork cracklings," answered Benjy. "Ma boils it to a thick mush. All our dogs get that."

His father rubbed Bugle Ann's head with his stubbled chin. "I puke out," growled the saturnine neighbor. "Spring, you're plumb foolish over that dog."

The older man shrugged. "I've run dogs

for seventy-odd year, but I never heard a voice like this. Nor did you, Cal, nor anybody else. She's galloped forty-five mile to-night. She's the sweetest-mouthed hound in Missouri, and sometimes I reckon I don't deserve her."

Baker asked, "What do you say about the fence, Spring?"

The other hounds were coming in—tan and white, wet ears, drooling jowls—a muddle of tails and snorts and sneezes in the firelight. Benjy took charge of the Davises. There were six of them out, this night, and he handled them with skill and deference and firmness ... his father still held Bugle Ann wrapped in his gaunt arms.

"I reckon," decided Spring, "that we'd better make a visit on this Jake Terry to-morrow. Call the Armstrongs and Lanceys and everybody together; even get the Pettigrews down from Big Panther Creek. Nobody has ever put up such a fence in these parts, and this is a mighty poor time to start."

Again Mr. Frank Mayor prayed for information.

"First place," explained Davis, "a fox hates such a fence. He's liable to shy off and leave the country because of it. But some of the foxes do like it, and that's even worse. Because a dog runs about fifteen mile an hour —and he hits a wove-wire fence in the dark. The fox is little—he's gone through without choking to death. The dog is liable to get killed."

He rubbed the home-made collar on Bugle Ann's neck. The collar plate was made from a silver dollar stamped flat, and silver dollars were none too plentiful with Springfield Davis any more.

"You can't get good hunting in a country where they put such fences across the fox range," Baker Royster summed up.

Bugle Ann was snoring happily in old Spring's arms.

Mr. Mayor had to drive all the way to Wolf Center, and he didn't arrive at home until four A.M., and his wife was worried to death. He told her that he had just attended the strangest fox hunt in the world; it was a kind of fox-hunting in which no killing took place. He was a discerning man, but in this case he spoke too soon.

The men of the Heaven Creek neighborhood waited upon Jacob Terry the next day.

3

THAT WAS June. By July, everybody knew that young Benjy Davis was tarnishing some mysterious code which existed among them all, and which no one of them could have explained or accounted for. Benjy was keeping company with Jacob Terry's daughter, and he made no secret of it.

She was named after her mother's people: Camden. She was eighteen, and she had the shaded hazel eyes of her mother's family, the dainty nostrils and firm lower lip which had marked the Camdens as quality folks when they first came to that country on horseback.

From her father Camden inherited the Terry stature, the Terry red hair. All Heaven Creek hoped that she hadn't inherited his surliness, loose tongue and ugly disposition. Benjy believed that she hadn't.

The crisis began to develop, one night when the grass still reeked from a July flood, and the southeast wind would have drowned any fox-smell which rose from last autumn's leaves. Springfield Davis sat on the front porch with his shoes off, and Bugle Ann dreamed on the step beside him.

Spring noticed that Benjy disappeared immediately after the evening chores were done, and later he smelled shoe polish. About eight o'clock Benjy came around the corner of the house, and he was wearing his good trousers and the blue necktie which Grandma Duncan had sent him for Christmas, and which he had never worn.

"It's a wet night," Spring said. He began to fill his pipe.

"I reckon the wind will change," said Benjy. "But anyway it's unlike to dry off the grass before midnight."

Spring put his hand on Bugle Ann. "If it does dry up enough, Cal will be out."

"I'll listen when I get back," Benjy told him. "If I hear you up in the woods, I'll come over. I thought," he said, "that I might go with Camden Terry to see the moving pictures in town."

McKee's Crossing was five miles to the north. . . . Spring thought, "I've counted, each time they was together. This is eight times." He said aloud, "That's a long way for a buggy. You plowed pretty steady all day, too."

"I wanted to lay-by that slow corn," Benjy said. "Camden can drive her Ford. We talked about it out in the field, when she came past to-day."

"Well," his father muttered. He thought, "So I was wrong. Nine times." He cleared his throat. "You might bring me a sack of Sweet Burley from town."

Benjy waved good-by. "I'll bring it," he

said, and went away like a war-chief in the dusk.

A long while later, Spring leaned down and blew softly against Bugle Ann's ear, and she roused up to wash his face for him. The April pups, by Billy Bryan out of Miss Wilson, came to tumble across his lap. "I reckon there would be no way to stop that," decided old Davis, "even if I wanted to. She looks more like the Camdens, and they was fine folks. Used to have a beautiful line of Irish-Maryland stock. I hope Benjy has sense enough to pay for the gasoline, if he rides in a Terry car. He will, though."

He sat for hours, thinking of Jacob Terry and how he had greeted the deputation which waited on him a few weeks before. They were men with sober faces, but they were not men who would shoot unless they were called by a certain name, and that was one curse which Jacob Terry had not dared to invoke. He had talked some of shooting dogs, but people didn't believe he really meant it. No man who had married a Camden could be perverted enough to shoot a fox-hound wantonly, they thought.

The fence was solidly in place: bull-strong, hog-tight and horse-high, just as the Royster boys had foretold. It ran across the creek, up the west slope of Heaven Hump, swung its yellow posts to the north and went down hill for another half mile. On the other two sides it paralleled Heaven Creek and Welsh Run. Jake Terry hadn't bought many sheep yet, but folks said that he was dickering here and there.

It seemed that recently he had inherited some money from an elderly aunt, and likely he would run through with that just as he had done with his wife's share of the Camden property.

When that woven belt of wire encompassed the slope of Heaven Hump, the Davises and Roysters had gone up into the woods and had dug out all the nearer fox dens. Several foxes were captured alive, and later were liberated miles away, east of the Armstrong farm. Their dens were broken in, or stopped with bowlders and saturated with chemicals. Now it was hoped that no fox would venture toward that menacing wire sash. The north range of Heaven Creek became a victory for Jacob Terry.

As a matter of fact, the foxes were quick to learn what Terry had done to the hills. Certain of them seemed to take a fiendish delight in slipping through the meshes, whereat the dogs would howl and scramble perilously, knotting themselves in the wire squares.

This night, Spring Davis dozed on the steps until after eleven, and his wife slept on the sofa in the living room. Mrs. Davis was thirty years younger than her husband, eighteen inches shorter, a few degrees less talkative, and she knew that after his dogs Spring loved her well.... The breeze did change, and when the old man awoke he found a steady west wind breathing its dryness against his face.

He went out into the yard and felt of the ground. He sniffed several times. Bugle Ann came behind him, stretching and yawning.

"I think a fox would hang on the high ground, after all. The scent'd be fairly free. Reckon you wouldn't have to grind your nose against the ground, little girl," said the master.

She swung her tail, and lifted her muzzle. "Now, hush!" he said, and waited with delight for her to disobey him.

She blew her trumpet.

"What is it?" called Mrs. Davis, sleepily.

The other hounds were answering, from out by the barn, and far in the southwest you could hear the Royster hounds casting about. "We had bugles in the rebel army," said Spring, "but I tell you, Adelaide, I waited a long time to hear the noise that this little girl has got snuggled inside her, all ready to let out when God is willing."

"Are you going up the creek?" asked his wife. They didn't say "down the creek" any more.

"I reckon I will. Cal is out. I hear General Bullard; sounds like he's striking. Will you fetch me a snack, while I get the lantern?"

She had a lunch ready when the old man came up from the corncrib, with his hands full of Frances Cleveland and Billy Bryan and Old Hickory. "I can't mind more than four, what with Benjy gone," he told Adelaide, and put his lunch in his pocket and the bugle under his suspender strap. He went across the cabbage patch, with the rest of the Davis dogs wailing their grief behind him.

"Poor little folks," he commiserated. "You'll just have to be patient, I reckon. Benjy sure is gone a long time. It must be a mighty good moving picture."

He saw the Royster lanterns opposite the

line fence, and he let the dogs loose, one by one. Bugle Ann shot into the lead. "You find the pack, little lady!" Spring shouted at her. "Find the pack if they come nigh. They got a long jump on you."

Cal Royster chuckled in the shadows. "Talk like she understood every word you said."

"I wager she'll be up with them inside thirty minutes," Spring responded. "And anyway, likely she does know what's what. How could she help it, with that silver cornet the Lord bequeathed her?"

Del and Thomas were off with the Lancey girls again, but Bake and old Cal and Spring Davis all waded Heaven Creek and went up on the south end of the Divide to build their fire. The bugs were bad, and it was more of a smudge than a camp-blaze.

"What's become of Benjy?" asked Bake, who knew well enough what had become of

Benjy. "Is he still taking that mail-school lesson about new ways of farming?"

"No, that's been done up for some time," Spring replied. He hesitated, then said: "He's gone to McKee's Crossing to the Wednesday night moving picture." This seemed neither the time nor the place to elaborate on his statement.

4

THE HOUNDS came down the valley soon after midnight, with the fox at a tantalizing short lead. The men descended the Divide when the baying sounded first from above them, and they felt rather than saw the truant varmint squeeze past them into the north.

White blur after white blur—like snowy hands whisking before the eyes—the dogs went by.

Cal Royster voiced the apprehension of the others when he spoke. "Fox'll go right up Chilly Branch Holler," he said, and Spring hoped that he was right, for it was hard to forget the menace of the wire which lay beyond.

They heard the dogs crossing Chilly

Branch near its mouth, and then Bugle Ann singled out ahead of them all, booming up the steep terraces of Heaven Hump. And Springfield Davis recognized another sound in the universe beyond: the faint clatter of an old Ford rocking along a narrow lane.

He thought, "So they're back from the moving pictures. I hope to God the fox switches east to the hill-top. The girl looks more like the Camdens than she does like Jacob. I reckon most of my dogs would be small enough to squeeze through that fence without getting hung up."

Then Bake cracked out, savagely, "They never went up the Hollow. Let's get over there!" and he lumbered away through the darkness. The two older men fumbled after him until their feet touched a deep cattle trail at the base of the hill, and then they could travel rapidly.

They splashed through the rapids near the mouth of Chilly Branch, and far ahead the hounds were rearing and yelling against Jacob Terry's hog-tight fence. One dog (he must have been Wound Stripe, and well-named, for Bake Royster swore about it) ki-yied, and told the world that an end of the wire had been sharp and gashing.

When the men reached the fence, waving their lanterns, the fox was long since gone. The pack danced and strutted in hysteria beside the barrier.

Wound Stripe's left fore-leg was drenched with blood.

"Bugle Ann ain't here," muttered Cal Royster.

The lantern beams had gone their anxious round.

"No," Spring Davis replied, "reckon she sailed right through." He walked up to the fence and tested its strength with his shoe, and prepared to climb over. You couldn't see his face in the lantern light.

Bake was thirty-four, and heavy enough,

but he was standing inside Terry's sheep pasture before old Springfield had managed to put his stiff legs astride the fence. Baker was thinking that Benjy should be there, and probably the others were thinking the same thing. . . . The far-away chugging of the Ford car had ceased, but a bright light moved rapidly toward them from the Terry farmhouse.

Sheep scampered here and there in distracted little coteries, appearing suddenly, and vanishing into the thick night amid a rattle of hillside pebbles.

"She'd come up to me, if she was inside the lot," said Spring. "It's possible she squeezed out at the other side, too."

Cal Royster put his arms in the fence meshes, trying vainly to stop their trembling. "She ain't giving voice no more. Maybe you better use your horn, Spring."

The old soldier had the bugle against his

lips when Jacob Terry loomed up the hillside, an electric flashlight in his fist.

"Get out of this pasture," Terry said. He did not yell, and there was added menace in his voice on that account.

"Look out," Cal Royster warned. He saw a shotgun in the curve of the farmer's arm.

Spring Davis turned around and took down the bugle. He rubbed a finger across his mouth. "Jacob," he said, "I come in here after my dog."

"If your damn dog is here, he's got no good business among my sheep." Terry held the flashlight steadily on old Springfield's face, and somehow Bake Royster thought of big searchlights he had seen weaving above the Argonne woods, on another night when hatred paraded on a grander scale.

Spring told Terry, "It's Bugle Ann. She wouldn't hurt your sheep, but she's small enough to come through your fence when a fox brings her here."

In the next silence, they listened for her voice, but could hear only the thudding of sheep which scampered along the slope. The rest of the dogs panted and mourned outside the fence.

"Get this straight, old boy." The flashlight held its unblinking stare in Terry's hand. "I'm gonna raise sheep, and I don't care a stink for all the dogs in Missouri. You keep yours off of my land, or they'll get a dose of Number Ten shot in the high end."

Benjy got there a moment later. He had left Camden at the lane entrance, and he had started across a spur of the Davis timber when he heard the hounds working straight down the creek. He had no lantern; the woods were black, so was the creek valley, and it had taken him longer than he anticipated.

Somehow there had been a menace in the entire evening, from the moment when Camden first cried against his clean green shirt.

He asked, "What's the matter?" and his

voice sounded like a youth's voice, breaking as it essayed the inflection. He snatched Cal Royster's lantern and investigated the hounds outside the pen. "Pa," he called, "where's Bugle Ann?" and then he came over.

Terry took a couple of steps closer. "There's more than just dogs that give me a peeve, anyway, and you know what I mean. Get out, all of you, and don't bend down my fence when you go over it, neither."

"One of my hounds got cut open," said Bake Royster. "I don't reckon you could be decent enough to staple down those ragged ends of wire, could you? Well, I'll sure come around and staple them for you."

Terry called him a name, and turned the muzzle of the gun toward him, but Benjy stepped out to meet it. He swung wide and openly, for he was not a trained boxer, but he was quicker than a cat in any movement. His fist lifted Terry off his heels and threw him heavily.

The shotgun flew wide; it was still un-cocked, and that kept it from going off.

"Take care, Benjy," was all his father said. There were grief and resignation in Spring's voice.

Terry rolled over and got up on his haunches.

"Don't you make a pass at me!" Benjy cried. "If you've killed Bugle Ann, I'll sure kill you."

"No," Spring said, "that'd be my job. But he hasn't, Benjy, he hasn't.... I'm plumb certain she went out the other side." Then, all in an instant, he stepped back and flung his arms high; one hand held the bugle.

He appealed, huskily, "For God's sake, listen to that!"

... She was far beyond Heaven Hump, far in the timber that blanketed Welsh Run. And she must have passed successfully through the north fence of Terry's pasture, for she had found the fox-smell again, and she was telling the whole state of Missouri about it.

It was a bugle, and every man knew that he would never hear its like again after she died.

Bake Royster had Terry's shotgun, and Benjy had his flashlight, and together they eyed the big farmer. "Terry," said Bake, "it's mighty fortunate for you that she's out there running safe and sound."

"You talk smart enough," whispered Jacob Terry. "Four against one! It's easy to talk smart."

"Your having this gun kind of evened it up."

"I'll even up any of your dogs, if they come on my land again." He went on to say what kind of dogs they were.

The hunters returned across the fence— all except Benjy.

"Come on, boy," Spring ordered him.

"Here's your light," said Benjy to Jacob.

"I reckoned you had something else to say."

Terry came close to him. "I'm not afraid of no Davises," he bellowed, "but I like to choose my friends! Don't you come near Camden no more—hear me? I'm particular about who my little girl goes places with."

"I reckoned that was it," replied Benjy. The others knew from the drawl with which he spoke that he was enraged almost beyond control. "Well, you can go to hell and fry in your own lard. You know well enough that fox-hounds don't go around pulling the hide off of sheep."

The man's voice rose in one shouting shriek. "Why, you young blacksnake, I'll kill every God damn cur that steps on this grass!"

"Jacob," Spring called to him, steadily enough, "I can't speak for the Roysters or Lanceys or Armstrongs or anybody else. But if you shoot a Davis dog, I'll blow you clean to glory. Now come out of that hog-pen, Benjy Davis."

Benjy climbed over the fence. Terry turned off the flashlight, and stood there like the black stub of a tree, watching him. "How about my gun?" he asked. "Are you folks going around stealing honest people's guns, too?"

"Here," said Bake. He clicked the breech and threw something far into the valley. He passed the shotgun back through the fence. "Both barrels empty. If you look careful, down by the creek, you'll maybe find the shells."

"Remember what I said!" yelled Jacob Terry. "I got an old cistern needs filling in, and I'd just as soon fill it up with dog-meat."

Spring Davis said nothing more, but Cal Royster spat out his tobacco and declared that nobody would forget a word that had been said. He doubted Spring Davis's ability to blow Jacob Terry to glory, and remarked

that another destination would be more easy
to promise.

They gathered up the dogs and went back
to the Divide. Their fire was nearly out, but
Bake soon kicked it into activity, and his
father found some dry wood stowed away in a
hollow basswood at the head of the ravine.

They waited until two-thirty o'clock, and
still Bugle Ann didn't come back, nor did they
hear her metal baying any more. Baker took
all the Royster dogs home to their straw beds,
and then returned to the fireside. The Davis
animals lay near the fire and sprawled like the
dead, as only hounds can ever do, but there
was a nervousness haunting their dreams, and
you could imagine that the eldest of them
moaned in his sleep for Bugle Ann.

Benjy sat like bronze, his arms locked
around his knees. From where he watched,
Cal Royster studied him and wondered if a
strain of Shawanee had not been dropped
into the Davis blood a century before....

The whisky got lower and lower in Cal's flask.

Spring Davis walked up and down outside the firelight, tramping a path from the basswood to the nearest clump of hickory sprouts. Once he came back to the fire and spat into the coals.

"Wonder how far the gamest fox would travel, if he set his mind to go in a bee-line?" he asked, but Cal Royster couldn't tell him. Then Spring climbed to the highest point of the Divide, and awakened the dozing whip-poor-wills with his urgent bugle.

5

IN THE darkest half-hour, immediately before the sky above the Armstrong farm turned gray, the men heard Jacob Terry's Ford beginning to hiccough. By that time they were scattered far and wide through the hills, but Bake Royster was on top of the Divide. He saw the car lights twist out of Terry's barnyard, and stop for awhile, and then go on, smudging away toward the county road.

Bake listened until the car had chugged in the direction of McKee's Crossing. He had started back toward the fire, when a gnome with a lantern waylaid him at the edge of the timber.

"Bake," whispered his father's voice, "I heard a yip."

He asked, "What kind of a yip?" with the unreasoning annoyance of a young man who shuns the mumbling vagaries of the aged.

"A dog yip," said Cal. "I was down the crick, plumb inside Terry's pasture again. And I heard it, up toward the house."

"Just once?"

In the growing fog of dawn, the old man clutched Baker's arm; his fingers tightened and relaxed. "The dog was struck dead, if you ask me. Terry might of done it with an ax, so's Spring wouldn't hear the gun."

Far along the upper twist of Chilly Branch Hollow, Spring Davis's bugle chanted stubbornly.... Bake felt stuffed up inside, as he considered what his father had just told him. "Benjy went to take his dogs home, Pa. You wait here for Spring, and I'll go for Del and Tom."

"Don't bring 'em back direct," commanded his father. "Send Tom across fields for the Lanceys, and have Del take the car and go up to the Armstrong place. He can ring the Pettigrews from there. I wish to God I was rich and could afford a telephone."

Bake swallowed. "You want the whole tribe?"

"We can't go off half-cocked, boy. Maybe it was just a notion I had, or something. I would of sworn it was a yip—just one quick one. Don't you dare tell Spring about it. But if that little bitch—"

"Lady," muttered Bake, not realizing he had said it.

"If she's hung up on bob-wire somewhere, we got to find her soon. It'll take a sight of searching. She never was one to try and dig up a fox-hole. Maybe she got clear over east on the slab, and some foreigners picked her up in a car."

Bake started for home like a good soldier, with crisp obedience in his mind. At all this talk of killing, he began to tremble inside with a nervousness which had never possessed him

since his discharge from the U. S. Veterans'
hospital in 1921. *Too much* ... his big feet
found the trampled mire beside Heaven Creek
... *too much of that sort of thing.* Just now
he didn't like the name Springfield. It didn't
make him think of a town there in Missouri,
but it did make him think of a rifle. Cartridges began to glint in his mind: pointed
clips of them, clicking one against the other
in a webbed pouch.

Suddenly, he thought he could feel the
cold solidity of a Springfield bolt in the curve
of his right index-finger.

He decided, "She's got to be caught in the
wire somewhere. It'll be the best thing that
could happen."

He routed Tom and Delbert out, and sent
them flying. His mother and Lucy stood in
their nightgowns and stared at him with cold,
pale eyes, and said they'd do the milking if
the men weren't back in an hour and a half.
... There was a mess of cornmeal in the

smelly summer kitchen, stirred up in a huge crock, and Bake took it out to the hounds. Halfway to the barn, he imagined that he heard a frightened voice yapping: "I'm runner—Brigade Headquarters—where's Sixtieth Infantry?" and the rifle bolts clicked in a machine-gun chorus. His throat was dusty, and he smelled pepper in his nose, as if some one had given him a blow that fractured the little blood vessels inside. . . . Then he pulled his nerves together, and went on to feed the dogs.

On the Divide behind his farm, Spring Davis came back to the dead fire with the sunrise smoking behind him. He walked, not like an old man who has been up and on his feet all night, but like a solemn pontiff who has sat in the cruelest judgment.

"It's the first time she ever disobeyed the horn," he said to Cal Royster and Benjy, who were waiting for him.

Cal kicked his empty bottle into the ashes.

"Spring, you ought to drink at least a cup of coffee and maybe have a snack, before you go further."

"Why," said Spring, "I don't need—"

Benjy said: "They'll be gathering at the house. Bake and Tom and Del are getting folks."

"I heard her," said Spring. "So did you. She had got through that second fence. I heard her plain, over past the outside of his pasture."

"Sure we heard her," crooned old Royster, "and if she ain't found by high noon—maybe just got a toe caught somewhere, or something, like when she was a pup—I'll give you a four-headed Shorthorn rooster!"

Benjy looked at his father. "Anyway, you got to stop by the house first."

Spring nodded. "Guess that's so. Come along with you."

Roy and Joe Lancey were sitting on the well-curb when they got to the house, and

Tom Royster was up at the kitchen door, talking with Mrs. Davis. The Lanceys stood up, awkwardly, as untutored men do at funerals, when Spring strode across the yard.

"Ma," asked Benjy, "you got some coffee?"

She nodded. "I kept hearing the horn, even after you was here, Benjy. The dogs have been just wild. I got a big coffeepot on the stove, and a couple skillets of eggs for anybody that wants them."

Bake Royster was coming across the south pasture, and another Lancey—Patterson, the sixteen-year-old one—was advancing up the front road on horseback.

At the back step, Spring Davis surveyed the men in his yard. His eyes were hot enough, but it was a slow and sturdy heat, infinitely ferocious. . . . An orange sun lifted above the Divide and found a whole jewelry store scattered over the clover behind the yard fence. All the remaining Davis dogs seemed to sense the import of this hour, except the April pups. They were smelling around Roy Lancey's legs.

"How about the ears on this one?" muttered Roy.

"They're well set," said Joe, "but she'll never have a stylish tail."

Cal Royster cackled, "Don't ask me! I ain't much on bench, but I'm the darndest Homeplate Judge you kids ever seen." The men all tried to laugh, as if he had said something very funny.

They heard the drone of the Armstrongs' old Studebaker from the road, and the rattle of Delbert Royster's Ford behind it. . . . When Spring Davis came out of the house five minutes later, there were thirteen men in the yard, including Benjy.

Spring had a lever action 30-30 Winchester in his hands. He tried it a couple of times, sliding shells into the breech, lowering the hammer with his thumb while he released the trigger, and flicking the cartridges out again.

The sun discovered the Winchester; for a moment its barrel looked like mother-of-pearl.

"I'd just as soon go alone," Spring said, mildly.

Benjy cried, "No."

"You might say I'd prefer it."

Benjy said, "I'll go with you."

Cal Royster tried to make an explosion of laughter, but it was only a vague squawl. "Why, of course we all got to go with you, Spring. It'll take all the men we can raise, to comb real thorough. Maybe that fox took her—" His throat crackled.

"Maybe the fox went clean to the Indian River," supplied young Tom, and there was a murmur of assent.

Spring clamped the rifle under his arm. "Very well, neighbors. . . . I might be wrong, but I reckon I can learn in a hurry when I get there." He stepped down into the yard. "Good-by, Mother," he said to his wife, and in the doorway she made a sound. The pups scampered to meet him, ears flopping and tails swinging. "Get 'em into the crib or kitchen or somewhere," he requested of the world, and kept going.

The unkempt mob of men started after him. Benjy hustled the pups into the kitchen, and his mother hooked the sagging screen door.

Down in the barn, Frances Cleveland began to bay, and her relatives took up the song. Benjy sprinted ahead and opened the plank gate for his father; the old man headed along the edge of the cornfield, but after twenty yards he struck off between the green fronds, his feet sinking deep into the damp earth and leaving the prints of his heel-corners bright and compressed.

The neighbors followed, all of them; they talked a little about corn. The thinnest corner of the Davis timber swayed forward to meet

them, and beyond that lay the lane, and beyond that the Terry house.

They came out into the jet lane, with its
golden, morning pools of mud and the
grooved ruts where Terry's Ford had plowed
through. Nobody tried to avoid the deeper
mire; the farmers marched in uneven phalanx
behind Spring Davis, and anybody would
have guessed that the old man didn't know
whether he was walking through mud or last
year's oat stubble.

Cal Royster had fallen to the rear, but not
through choice. A little pageant walked with
him, and impeded his footsteps ... it was
when he was eighteen, some fifty years earlier,
and the neighbors all went up Welsh Run to
prosecute Big Cass Strickland when he beat
his two children to death. They prosecuted
him at the end of his own wagon-harness,
wrapped around the limb of a white-oak tree,
and he hung there seven hours before any one
cut him down. . . .

You couldn't see a soul moving in the Terry yard, and now the men believed most certainly that Jacob Terry had gone far away in the Ford, before dawn. Bake Royster and his father began to watch for tracks, as soon as they came opposite the weed-grown orchard, and it was impossible for them to conceal their search.

Cal felt Spring Davis turning and staring at him, and he held his face closer than ever to the ground.

Then all the men had stopped. Benjy Davis came back and stood between the two Roysters, with his hands clamped over his hip-bones.

"The pack never got up this high," he said. "They weren't out of the creek valley, except on the other side."

"No," whispered old Cal. "We was just a-looking."

Benjy grabbed Bake's shoulder and turned him around. "What do you know, Bake?"

"It ain't me," said Bake. "It's Pa. He heard it. I didn't."

Cal stammered, "Now, Benjy Davis. My ears are mighty old and mighty tricky. I can't depend on them no way."

"You better speak up," drawled Benjy. Spring Davis had come back to stand beside them; the rest of the neighbors waited in uneasy silence beyond.

"Well," Cal told them, "it did sound like a yip."

"Up here?" persisted Benjy.

"It was kind of in this general direction. I guess it was a short while before sun-up."

Benjy turned to his father, and tried to take the gun. The old man pushed him away with sudden and amazing strength. "You remember, boy," he said, as if there wasn't another man within twenty miles, "how she got her foot caught in that rat-trap before she was weaned."

Bake Royster yowled, without being asked,

"Sure, sure! Everybody knows that. But one gone toe never bothered her, because it happened when she was young enough. You'd never pick her as belonging to a Casual Outfit."

"All right, Father," Benjy Davis said. Nobody had ever heard him say Father before. "I reckon any tracks that are here would be like cement in the mud. Quite—" He hunted for the word. "Quite unmistakable."

"I'll warrant you," his father replied. Spring drew down the lever of his Winchester the barest part of its arc: there was a shell in the breech. He clicked it back. Then he turned and started east along the lane, with his eyes boring against the ground.

Benjy looked at him as if he were just seeing him for the first time. "Wait," he cried, and the old man turned. Benjy brought out a sack of Sweet Burley, its blue seal blazing in the fresh sunlight. "I just remembered that you wanted me to bring this from town, and I been carrying it in my pants all this time."

Spring nodded. "I'm obliged, Benjy." He thrust the tobacco into his hip pocket. "Before Cal talked about that yip," he told his neighbors, "I had been quite divided. I thought that probably she was in wire, or else somebody had stole her, over on the slab highway. Just possibly."

They didn't find any tracks until they came to the yard gate, almost directly in front of the house. Then there were a few. The imprints were made by the feet of a hound coming from the east, coming slowly and wearily a few inches outside the thick grass which bordered the wood road.

Everybody moved off upon the turf, and let the Davises handle this matter in their own way.

Benjy stood looking into the deserted barnyard, but his father got down on his knees and examined the smoother patches of drying mud near the intersection of the wheel ruts.

"How about that toe?" asked the boy.

"I think so," answered Spring, haltingly. "I'm not right certain: so many car wheels, and other tracks. She must of turned off on the grass at this point.... Wait'll I find a good one."

Then at last he stood up, and took the rifle in both hands. "Oh, I reckon it would stand in court," he declared. "Just like fingerprints and such. That gone toe is as plain as copper plate. And the tracks don't pass this gateway. She did get this far, on the way home."

A drop of water bobbed over his crusty eyelid and spent itself in a quick streak on his face, dividing and splitting when it came to a nest of wrinkles.

Benjy said, "She was all alone, and likely the fox holed over in Lester's timber near the creek mouth. She knew this old wood road come back, and was easier traveling. She knew enough not to go through those wove-wire fences unless a fox took her that way."

"Cal Royster," said Spring, "you owe me a four-headed Shorthorn rooster." He faced the Terry house for the first time.

Old Ed Armstrong cried, "Now, Spring-field. Now, Brother, wait a spell! The Lord don't smile on wrath in unguarded moments of haste."

"You and the Lord can hold your horses," Spring said, without turning his head. "If I'm looking for rats in my granary, I don't set down and pray on it."

Benjy pleaded, "Give me that Winchester, Pa."

"Pshaw, scat," said his father, and started into the farmyard. "You never bred her, did you? She was mine."

Benjy swung around and glared at the neighbors. "He don't want to go in with a whole parade. I'll stay by this gate. Don't nobody try to come past me."

"Spring!" howled Cal Royster. "He's gone! Spring, I tell you he went away in the car. We all heard it go. We—"

"If he ain't at home," said Benjy, "Pa'll wait."

Jacob Terry came out on the kitchen porch. In the barn lot, his two cows were lowing: they had not yet been milked, and none of the neighbors was surprised to know that Jacob had put off his milking until that hour. There were young chickens on the porch, and in the yard below.

Terry held his shotgun in his hands; of course there had been plenty of other shells in the house. Number Ten shot, Baker remembered. Little bright lights flickered in Bake's eyes, and again he smelled that pepper of a painful smash against his nose.

"Get out of here, you old devil," said Terry.

"What'd you do with her?" asked Spring.

His tone was flat. "The tracks are to the gate. Did you haul her inside, then?"

Terry mouthed, "I never killed your damn dog, but I'll put some slugs through you if you don't get out of here." He began to hoist the shotgun toward his shoulder.

Springfield Davis fired from his hip. Terry dropped the shotgun and looked surprised and horrified; a dishpan behind him rang like a gong, and fell from its nail, rolling unsteadily across the floor of the porch. Terry's knees bent; he tried to get hold of his chest, and failed. He fell forward into the mud below the porch, with his arms doubled under him.

A lot of half-feathered chickens scurried away from him, peeping shrilly. When the men had rolled him over, they found that one chicken was dead beneath him—crushed flat when he fell upon it.

Benjy went into the house, but Camden wasn't there, and he was dumbly grateful—

even in this calamity, and in the mystery of
her absence. But the Ford was gone. She
must have driven away in it.

That afternoon, after Springfield Davis
had ridden to Wolf Center with the Sheriff,
the authorities were able to telephone to the
Camdens up in Jackson County. Camden
Terry had arrived there about noon, but had
driven on to an isolated farm belonging to a
bachelor uncle. It was twenty-four hours before she could be notified and could complete
the return trip as far as Wolf Center.

On the first day when people sat in the big,
hot room among the scarred oak desks, Benjy
Davis thought Camden looked prettier than
she had ever looked before. Her pallor was
the cold pallor of hepaticas; her eyes were
excessively deep and shaded and secret.

Benjy didn't look her way when he thought
she might be looking at him, but he studied
her often when she was watching old Spring
and the Coroner and the other people. Her

story was calm, distant, told without emotion
—it might have been translated from some
ancient book. Yes, she had been with Benjy
Davis the night before the shooting. Yes, she
knew that her father had had trouble with
the neighbors over his fence and their fox-
hounds. She knew that there had been threats.
...After her father came back to the house
from the sheep pasture, they had engaged in
an argument.

He had slapped her; just once, she said;
not very hard. She packed some clothes, and
took the Ford. He dared not stop her, because the Ford was hers—not his. Her Aunt
Nancy had given it to her after Uncle Newt
died; Aunt Nancy couldn't drive.

(She didn't look at Benjy, either, when
she thought that he might be observing her.
Sometimes their glances crossed, but never
seemed to meet and hold. Each understood
that Jacob Terry was still between them,
standing or lying dead, it didn't make any

difference. In a way, Spring Davis also was between them now. And Bugle Ann.)

Her voice continued soberly, a little-girl voice. She thought that she wouldn't stay with her father any more, after that night. She drove up to Jackson County, and went out to Uncle Elnathan's place, and that was where the news had reached her.

Benjy Davis and the Royster boys spent days in going over the Terry farm, both before and after the sale of farm animals and machinery and household goods. They couldn't find a trace of Bugle Ann's body, even though they took up wooden slabs and explored the old cistern. She could have been buried in any loose earth of the barnyard or hog-lot, and no one would have known the difference.

Spring Davis was tried in September; the trial was in no way notable except for the oration on fox-hounds by a young attorney who volunteered to assume the defense without pay. The young attorney quoted, "Senator Vest's Tribute to the Dog," and added tributes of his own. He discussed fox-hunting as practiced in Missouri, and offered a biographical sketch of Old Man Spaulding, who was still alive in those days. In the eastern part of these great United States, said the young attorney, fox-hunting was an Anglicized pose of the idle rich, and they had many strange fetishes, not the least of which was the custom never to refer to a fox-hound as a "dog." They were all "hounds." Most of his listeners thought that very odd, but they did remember with interest how Spring Davis always called his female dogs Little Ladies or Little Girls.

Fifty years before, certainly, he would never have been convicted. But in this age you must not kill a man, even when another man talks of shooting and has a shotgun in his hands. It was proved that Spring Davis went into the Terry yard armed and ready to kill——he said as much himself. It was proved that Jacob Terry did not fire the first shot, nor did he have his gun at his shoulder when he was struck down.

The most important *corpus delicti*—the body of Bugle Ann——was not available. In short, no one could swear beyond all doubt that Jacob Terry had killed her. Spring Davis had usurped the prerogatives of the Sovereign State of Missouri, and the Sovereign State of Missouri brought that out very pointedly.

Girls made fudge for Spring while he was in jail; women sent in basket dinners. He gave the fudge away, of course, and some of the dinners. There was muttering at his conviction, and men talked darkly of a jail delivery. But such a rebellion belonged fifty years in the past. Springfield Davis went to Jefferson City and served three years, eight months and twenty-one days, and then he was pardoned by the governor.

6

DURING THE first June which Spring
spent in prison, the voice of Bugle Ann came
back to ring across the dark valleys. Adelaide Davis was the first to hear this banshee,
and she ran and told Benjy, and then they
were both awake. Over on the next farm, Cal
Royster started from his bed screaming,
"Bake! Bake! It's her—" and even the
youngest Lancey, who was up with a tooth-
ache, declared that there was no mistake in
the identity.

And from that night rose the sprout of a
legend which spread itself over the whole
county, and farther than that. It was the
legend of a white dog—lean, like hounds of
the Spaulding line—who bugled her way
through the brush at night, who ran with

her head high, calling and hunting for the master who had been carried away from the hills he loved.

They said she ran at the head of a silent pack in which there were thirty-hour dogs, all the great and noble sires who had galloped those ranges before the Civil War. There were the hounds brought into Missouri when Daniel Boone came, great swordmouthed brutes who could pull down a deer if they wanted to. But they all ran silently— their feet made not even a whisper in the dryest leaves of last year, and their baying was not the kind which ordinary people could hear. Only if you were about to die, you might hear them crying all at once.

But the Davises and the Roysters and one Lancey, and even Old Ed Armstrong's hired man—all had heard Bugle Ann on that solitary night, and though they didn't hear her again, it was said that Benjy Davis spent more hours roving the woods than was wise for a young man with a farm on his hands.

No one lived at the Terry farm now. Shortly after Springfield Davis had gone to the penitentiary, men from McKee's Crossing came and took down the hog-tight wire fence. When questioned, they declared that a lawyer had told them they could have the wire and posts if they'd take them down. It was easy to pry out the staples, and they bore the wire away in huge rolls atop their trucks. But the posts were another matter; they quit digging after they had uprooted a few. Still, the wire was the main thing.

And there were those who swore that the pack led by Bugle Ann could go through a hog-tight fence like so much dishwater, but young Benjy Davis was hard to convince. After he had searched and yelled through every ravine between the Indian River and Big Panther Hollow, he declared that it had all been a mistake. Bugle Ann lay somewhere beneath the fresh weeds that grew in Terry's hog-lot, and as for her baying—it was another dog, that was all.

"It was her," insisted Adelaide Davis. "If your Pa had been here, he would of got up out of bed and gone for his lantern."

"Well," said Benjy, "I did that, didn't I?"

"But she quit giving voice," his mother said, "and whoever stole her took her away again." Her hands shook, in their cerements of bread dough. "Or else—"

He chided, awkwardly, "I got to get out to the field. . . . It's mighty unnatural to believe in ghosts."

Then he returned to his cultivator seat, and combed the black earth of the cornfield; he combed the rows early and late, and this year he had planted extra acreage. It was too bad, perhaps, for the price of corn got lower—so low that Benjy said there was no sense in selling. He didn't sell his corn, but he did sell the April pups of the year before, to the Lanceys. He took a corn-crib in payment—one fairly new. They moved it over to the Davis place with teams and cables and turnstiles: a three-day job. The Davises were hard put to scratch for a living, and that new corn-crib did look like a lot of foolishness.

Benjy stored his 1933 corn, too, and then came the next summer and the drouth, and corn at seventy cents. . . . Benjy carried an important slip of pink paper out of the office of the Wolf Center Farmers' Grain Company, and shoved it under a grille at the Wolf Center Savings Bank.

Mr. Mayor came after him and talked of insurance, but the only expenditures which Benjy was known to have made were subscriptions to *The Red Ranger* and *The Hunter's Horn*. You couldn't expect the library at the state prison to have those periodicals in stock.

It was the night of Wednesday, September 26th, when Bake Royster came around to the Davis place and got Benjy out of bed. Bake could remember the date forever; that day, sixteen years removed, marked the opening of the Meuse-Argonne offensive. Bake had a great head for names and dates.

He looked green around the gills when Benjy padded out across the kitchen in his night-shirt, and wanted to know what was up.

"I've found something," announced Bake. "Found it in the dark, and I guess you better come and see it."

Benjy's sharp glance made a hole in Royster's face. "I'll get my clothes, Bake. Keep soft, so's not to wake Ma. Her sciatica has been bothering her again."

He came out promptly, and sat on the back step to draw on his shoes. "Where is this— what you found?"

"It's clear in the east side of Bachelor's timber, where the Bachelor used to have a shack. It's a smart piece, but I got my lantern."

"I better take mine, too," said Benjy. He brought a square, scarlet-enameled electric lantern from the porch shelf; Bake thought of that check for the seventy-cent corn.

They went across the yard, with the white disk dancing around their feet and ahead of them. "Maybe you'll want a spade, too," muttered Bake.

"A spade?" Benjy stopped and looked at him in the dark.

Bake said, "Or else a grain sack."

After a moment, Benjy replied, "I'll get a sack, I think," and he found one hanging inside the barn door. Together they crossed the garden patch, and up across the Divide they could hear the Royster dogs and a couple of Armstrongs working intently north into the tangles along Chilly Branch. One or two of the Davis hounds wailed at them, but half-heartedly: the Davis hounds had forgotten what a black-dark night was like, with a fox spraying his oily perfume through the thickets.

"Wound Stripe and Toul Sector had him across the corner of Bachelor's," explained Royster. "Some young dogs was along with them, and that little Elsie Janis got herself twisted in some rusty wire. That's how I come to go down there and—"

He gargled in the dimness, and added with an attempt at being casual, "Tom and Pa are there now."

When they crossed Heaven Creek (its widest pool could have flowed between your shoes, after the drouth) Baker began to remonstrate with Benjy Davis.

"I don't see what ails you, Benjy. It's a shame to have good stock tied up and molting away the way yours are."

"You can't sashay around the woods all night, if you're busy farming," the younger man told him.

Bake growled, "Now, I know all about that

corn! You don't need to rub it into me. But
you ain't had nothing but dried-up crops to
worry you, this year, and since the fall rains
began to come there's been *beaucoup* fox
around here."

For awhile Benjy climbed the incline without speaking, loose pebbles rolling down
around Bake Royster as he plodded an arm's
length behind. "No stomach for it," Benjy
said, at last, and Baker knew that was really
the explanation. "Not until he's out of that
damn place. I can't set beside a fire and listen to the baying, and know he's at Jefferson
City in a cell-house."

It was eerie, passing through the oak
woods, with a few katydids throbbing in
secret dens under the stiff green leaves, and
occasional yellow leaves sailing down into the
straight electric ray. There was a feel of
frost in the air, and Bake kept thinking of
what he had found an hour before... a dog
like Bugle Ann could take a thousand ghost

hounds across the prairies among the stars, and still her baying would come back to you. Bake had ceased worrying about Springfield rifles and cartridges in webbed pouches, long before; sometimes still he thought of Jacob Terry and the chicken which had been crushed beneath his tumbling body, and he wouldn't get enthusiastic about half-feathered chickens ever again, especially if they made a shrill peeping.

But the death of Jacob Terry had come with its own certain violence, justified and canceled by a rifle bullet, the same as the many deaths Baker had seen in the valley of the Meuse. In Bugle Ann's passing there was too much mystery for any man to ponder. Any man who had ever been a patient in a government hospital.

The Bachelor's cabin was nothing but a heap of mossy shingles and broken crockery among the hickory saplings, for the Bachelor had left the country before Bake Royster was born. Some of his wire existed still: thick, old-fashioned plaits of bent rust amid the stumps. And near one of those barricades Cal Royster and young Tom waited with their lantern.

"Pa," called Bake.

"I'm right here," said the old man. "Evening, Benjy." Tom Royster didn't offer any greeting; embarrassment had frozen him into silence.

Benjy stood beside them and took what Cal Royster handed him. It was a leather collar, now stiff as iron with winter and summer and rain and mold, but the flattened silver dollar on it was unmistakable—you could even scrape away what had gathered over it, and see the Liberty head all flatly distorted, with its crudely-scratched legend.

The men waited silently.

"Where's the rest?" asked Benjy, after a long time. He slid the collar, with leaves still clinging to it, inside his shirt.

"Right here, in the bushes. They're a little scattered."

Benjy got down on his knees. If you had seen him, and had not known why he was there, you would have thought that he was praying. . . . Cal Royster had a vague notion that he ought to remove his hat, but Cal had never done such a thing for a dog.

"How long would you say?" asked Benjy presently.

The others murmured, hazarding several opinions. You couldn't tell much about bones. Maybe a doctor could. Animals had been there, probably, and birds. Maybe a year, maybe two, or three, or—

It was the collar which first had attracted Bake's attention. He saw it sticking up out of the leaves while he was releasing Elsie Janis from the wire. The young hound had left some of her blood there, from a lacerated elbow, and it seemed strangely appropriate to have that ground moistened with the blood of a fox-hound, even if she wasn't a Davis dog.

"The point is," said Benjy, speaking slowly and gravely, "whether she was here all the time, that night, or whether she come later. Somehow or other. The point is whether we heard her voice two year ago last June, or whether—"

Cal Royster said, "By God, it was her voice. Reckon I heard it."

"And by God," whispered Benjy, "those were her tracks at the edge of Terry's barn-yard, in July of 'thirty-one."

"So what?" asked young Tom. It was slang such as he always picked up at the moving pictures, but it seemed unusually apt.

Benjy said, "I reckon there's nothing I can do except tote her home in the grain sack. I'm glad I didn't bring the spade, Bake, be-cause now I'd be tempted to use it: just seem like a lot of old sticks, somehow, and I always did think a dog skull was powerful ugly."

They helped him pick up the relics, and he carried them back home while Bake Royster went ahead with the electric lantern. The men brought a shovel from the woodshed and buried the fragments, grain sack and all, beneath the sweet-crab tree at the corner of Mrs. Davis's little orchard. Benjy washed the collar and wiped it clean, using several dish towels in the process, and then he took it upstairs and hung it over the pointed, upright support of his bureau mirror, on top of his five neckties.

He told his mother the next morning, and of course through the Roysters the story was well around the neighborhood before noon. But Benjy and his mother were positive that no word of it would reach the ears of Springfield Davis at Jefferson City, and they were correct. It was the sort of a tale which might not be welcomed in print, so the *Weekly Clarion-Advocate* held no mention of it. No person except members of the family carried

on any correspondence with Spring Davis,
anyway, and thus the old man did not learn
of how Bugle Ann's skeleton had been found
until after he was released from prison.

It gave Bake Royster a fever, however, and
he spent four days in bed. His family
thought it was a kind of flu, but Baker knew
the truth. He'd lie there at night, until he got
over it, and watch the whole insane puzzle
exploding before his eyes. Desperately he
tried to align the formations—to put each
separate element in the nook where it belonged; and this was lunacy to attempt.

Camden Terry: take her, now. She was
living up in Jackson County, folks said, and
she had never offered to sell the farm. Just
let it grow to weeds. Nobody seemed to know
whether or not she was married, and natu-
rally it would take a hardy soul to mention
her name to Benjy. Bake reckoned that
Benjy had been mighty sweet on Camden.

Everybody had seen the tracks at Jake

Terry's gate; there was no doubt about that
missing toe. Not another hound in the neighborhood had a toe gone. So there were her
tracks, and why would Bugle Ann have gone
across Heaven Creek from the Terry farm—
why would she have climbed Heaven Hump,
or gone through Chilly Branch Hollow, and
south into the timber land to get herself
strangled in the Bachelor's wire? Spring
Davis was making the hills quiver with his
trumpet, and people all knew how Bugle Ann
would come to such a summons.

No, she must have lived somehow, somewhere—and then she must have come back to
the woods she loved, on another night, in
June of 1932. Then they had heard her calling, and then she had met her death, alone
beside the windfall of curling shingles.

No, she must have been a ghost, all along.
It was not natural for any dog to have a voice
like hers, and perhaps she had been sired by
one of the silent pack which followed her so

willingly in popular imagination. Even now her bones lay wadded in the Davis orchard, but Bugle Ann was up and gone, baying in ranges where no horns could ever summon her, and it would be death to hear her bugling again.... It was this surmise, however hysterical, which comforted Baker Royster and let him sleep with no more fever. Yet it was hard for him to forget how Benjy Davis had looked in the lantern light, coming down from the Divide with that sack of bones swinging from his shoulder and Bugle Ann's collar nestling inside his shirt.

7

THEY HAD less than twenty-four hours'
warning, the next June when Springfield
Davis was sent home from the penitentiary.
There hadn't been such a tornado of fes-
tivity in the neighborhood since Delbert Royster and LaVonne Lancey were married two
years before, and even then the Davises could
not have felt very festive.

At five-thirty P.M. of the great day, Benjy
and Bake started for McKee's Crossing in
the old Royster car, but the fan-belt parted
and as a result the train was just pulling out
when they careened up to the station. They
saw Spring Davis sitting there with a straw
suitcase beside him.

His hair and mustache were snow-white
and his face sagged, as if its fleshy sub-struc-

ture had dried up. His pointed shoulders came forward more noticeably and tried to meet across the front of his chest, but otherwise his appearance was the same as it had been. Benjy expected him to be as pale as a tallow candle, but he was not; Spring explained later that he had worked out of doors a good deal. The worst thing about the whole prison experience, he thought, was having so many of the convicts call him Pop.

He was eighty-six years old, and walked stiffly, and sometimes he'd open his mouth for a moment before he could say anything when he wanted to talk.

They got him into the car, with twenty townspeople staring quietly at him, and started for home. Spring didn't talk much on the way. He took off his old slouch hat and let the wind blow his hair—soft as milkweed silk. Once he said, "I see they've cut down that willow-row on the Collins place," and again, "Well, there's no use in my not saying that I was surprised—terribly surprised. It come so sudden! I didn't expect them to let me out for years and years."

He glanced keenly toward the Terry place as they passed its burdock-grown lane, and he seemed about to ask a question. But the next moment the north field of the Davises had swum past, and the car was crunching in at the gate. Adelaide Davis was just opening the screen door: others of the neighborhood women huddled behind her, and a lot of men were squatting on their heels beneath the cottonwood tree. Benjy always remembered how Cal Royster snapped his knife shut and put it into his pocket before he turned. Cal had been whittling a toy dart for one of the Lancey kids.

A long table had been arranged beside the peony bushes, and you could smell everything from fried chicken to beet pickles. After the greetings were made, Spring said that he'd like to put on some other clothes, and Benjy went behind him as he toiled up the narrow stairway to the hot rooms under the eaves. Spring's old work-clothes were there, but washed and smooth and foreign to him; he would not feel at home until his crooked knees and elbows had made their appropriate dents in the cloth.

Mrs. Davis had disposed of his old suspenders, and he couldn't get a satisfactory adjustment on the ones he was wearing. He came into Benjy's room for help, and the first thing he saw was Bugle Ann's collar hanging beside the mirror.

If he lived to be a hundred, Benjy would never cease blaming himself for that.

Finally, after working his mouth for a long time, Spring managed to say, "Then you did find her. You never wrote it to me."

"Pa," Benjy groaned, "now you set down, Pa. Set down." And at last the old man sank deep into the narrow feather-bed.

He wanted to know, "Where was it?
Where?"

"Up in Bachelor's timber. We never found
her until last September."

"Bachelor's," echoed Spring. And then:
"No, no, couldn't have been there."

"It was right beside the old shack," said
his son, as gently as he could.

Spring stared for awhile. Downstairs they
were yelling and laughing, and LaVonne
Lancey Royster was ringing a dinner bell.
Out in the yard, old Billy Bryan began to
challenge with excitement.

"Then Terry never did it," said Spring.

"Maybe she run up there—after he shot
her—or—"

The old man hissed, "Ah, stop your foolish
talk!" His eyes were wet and blazing. "Nev-
ertheless," he declared in a rapid whisper,
"I'm thankful I done it when I did, for certainly I'd had to do it sometime. He meant it,
Benjy. He would of killed her in a minute."

"Sure he would!" cried Benjy. "You don't think anybody in this world is blaming you, do you?"

Springfield had the collar in his hand, turning it slowly around and around.

Benjy mopped his perspiring forehead. "Pa," he began, "that ain't the whole story. There was a time, first June after you went up there—"

He told briefly of the dog's bugling which had echoed in the woods beyond Heaven Creek, and how the neighborhood had taken it, and of the phantom pack which was said to hunt so silently at night, unattended by any hunters.

Spring blew his nose when Benjy was through. "There was a time when I would of laughed my head off at that," he said, simply enough, "but I've had plenty time to think, these last four years. There were funny things in the War, boy, and there's been funny things other times. My mother knew that brother Rufus was killed by a snapped log-cabin, long before they ever brung her the news. She saw it in a kind of dream.... I don't say you heard Bugle Ann up there in the timber, that night, but you did hear something. Mighty often I thought I heard her, clear off in Jefferson City."

Then they went downstairs and out into the yard, to the fried chicken and other food, and all the talk, and all the people.

Supper stretched far into the dusk; then the table was cleared, and women began chattering and packing their baskets in the vicious heat of the kitchen. The men sat on the front porch and on the grass, and children shrieked at mysterious games among the berry bushes.

They had tried to enthrone Springfield Davis in the big splint-bottomed rocker, but he preferred to sit with his angular spine against a porch post. The dogs came to pay their respects; there was no one of them that he loved well enough to let it sleep **across his** lap, though Benjy watched hopefully.

In the first hush of twilight, when conversation had labored away from fox-hunting a dozen times, Spring astonished the crowd by rising to his feet and walking slowly down into the yard to feel the grass.

"It's not real wet," he said, so distinctly that all could hear him, "but there's a promising feel of dampness between the blades. When did it rain here?"

Somebody coughed. "Must of been night-before-last."

The pipes and cigarettes glowed spasmodically, and in the kitchen the younger Lancey girls were trying to harmonize with *Sometimes I'm happy, sometimes I'm blue.*

"This night'll be black-dark and that's a fact," came from Cal Royster.

Spring stood listening to the girls' song. "Radio," he muttered. "Well, we had radio music up there, too." He called to Royster,

"Cal, I've been smelling at black-dark nights for nigh onto four years."

"I didn't think you'd feel—" Bake started to say, and then he chewed his nervous lip.

Spring Davis echoed, "Feel what?" He looked like a tall, guerrilla ghost in the thickening dusk, and the scent of June flowers was heavy as at a funeral. "Why, when a relative dies we all go on living, don't we? We all have to. I'd like, just as quick as possible, to set beside a fire again."

Benjy stood up. He felt his knees quivering. "The dogs are rusty, Pa. You know I've been farming pretty steady."

"They'll get the kinks out of their noses, once a fox is good and sweet," said Spring. It was as if he alone were trying to whistle up the courage of his neighbors. "I hate to see a good, sticky night go to waste. And there ain't any southeast wind."

There was a stir among the farmers, and more than one stood up. But for all their eagerness a certain delicacy possessed them now. They realized that this pathetic rite—the first journeying of old Spring to the hills of Heaven Creek—was something sacred to the Davises and Roysters, who had hunted together time out of mind.

"I'm afraid Gabe won't look after that colt proper," said old Ed Armstrong. "Awful hard to keep a hock bandaged." The Lanceys spoke of a big day in the field to-morrow, and Henry Pettigrew made lugubrious mention of his rheumatic knee.

"Well," Bake Royster announced, in a sweeping gesture of exclusion, "looks like everybody else has to go home and do chores or go to bed early, but Pa and I might trail up in the timber a spell with you, Spring."

Davis said, "Fetch the hounds, Benjy. I don't reckon we'll need a snack to-night, we're so full of good supper."

In half an hour the four of them had crossed the narrow clover field and were wading the valley darkness: Spring, Benjy, Cal and Baker. A solid bank of clouds rose slowly out of the west, and rain would come before morning. The air was one great, mossy cellar of humidity.

On the high crest of the Divide, the hounds went loose—four Davis dogs and five Roysters. All of the Davis dogs were elderly hounds whose voices Spring Davis knew as well as his own name. The white blots went speeding, zigzagging toward the shadows where foxes most often made their path.

The men sat on their haunches and waited.

"One's struck," said Cal, when a haunting moan came from the hilltop. The moan stopped suddenly. "No," Benjy grunted, "you just thought so. If that was Toul Sector ... has he run on his own trail lately, Bake?"

Bake grinned, in spite of himself. "Not for a good month. Wait awhile."

The insects skirmished around them. At

last little Elsie Janis found exciting evidence; she talked about it. Billy Bryan and Old Hickory joined her, and the whole mob went hooting melodiously toward the south slope.

"Good voice she's got," said Spring. "She one of your new ones, Cal?"

"Just small fry," replied Royster, with pride which he couldn't conceal, "and she'll run as long as a fox makes tracks."

Baker thought, "Good voice? Well, the old guy said so," and yet Bake was well aware that her yelps were not qualified for a chorus of the best Royster voices, let alone to bring praise from the man who had bred Bugle Ann. He wondered whether it was merely a mistaken kindness on Spring's part, or whether the old man had really lost his ear. Three years, eight months and twenty-one days were an awful long time.

Bake began to hum *I stood in the jail-*

house, and stopped in horror when he realized what he was humming.

He heard the bubbling of his father's whisky bottle. "Let's have a fire," Cal ordered.

The first curling flame, nursed tenderly through drying twigs, showed Benjy Davis something which made him catch his breath. He had to build the fire higher before he was sure. . . . Yes, old Springfield had gone upstairs before he left the house, but Benjy hadn't given it any thought at the time. And now he saw that the old man wore the battered bugle, tucked neatly beneath his suspender strap.

Stiff little needles rose on Benjy's scalp. He kept fooling with the fire.

"They're well toward Big Panther Holler," Cal estimated.

Spring inclined his head critically. "Yes, that's a bee-line fox to-night. Doesn't let no crops grow under his feet." He spoke without a tremor of madness, but his old bugle glowed and shimmered and caught dull flashes from the firelight at every snap of the flames.

Then Benjy saw the shaking of Baker Royster's hands, and he knew that Bake too had seen the trumpet.... The son thought crazily, "Christ in the Mountains, what would we do if he stood up and started to blow that thing?"

Bake was shivering with the same wonder. This was June ... he knew the month, and the year, and the farm—he knew every scrap of sod beneath his feet—and yet the first blast of that horn would turn the commonplace world to madness. No person could estimate what tribes might come sweeping through the underbrush in answer.

After a few moments, it was impossible to hear the dogs any more. They had gone deep into the crooked defile of Big Panther Creek; there was no telling just when they might return. The Roysters knew this fox well enough: their dogs had run him frequently during the year. He was a bee-liner from the word Go, as Cal often remarked, and he'd just as soon venture into the next county as not. But always he holed at the south end of Bachelor's timber, so they knew the pack would come howling back eventually.

No one talked. The log on the fire shrank to the thinness of a charred bone, and Benjy arose to see whether he could find another one dry enough to burn. There was a V of discarded fence posts nearby, and under their shelter perhaps—

He stopped, frozen in his tracks as the sound pierced him. It was a faint and elvish cry, half lost amid the buzz of tree-toads, and it might have been fathered by one of those night-hawks which rode high overhead.... Still, it never came from the throat of a bird, and in the first second Benjy wondered what sort of a throat it had come from.

Before the sudden blurring of his gaze, he

watched his father's head lifting, nodding. Spring's mouth had opened slightly, in the reflex of one who listens without half knowing....

Again the thin, silver measure—the horn of something which searched the forest away over beyond Heaven Hump. Bake Royster crawled up on his elbow, and his face became yellow instead of red in the firelight.

"Benjy," whispered Spring Davis, "I reckon she's struck."

The young man made a harsh sound. "It's a dog," he said. "Fox-hound that belongs to— Running all off by himself, that way. I reckon he's an Armstrong."

The sockets beneath Spring's eyebrows were blank and dark and empty; the weaving shadows did strange things to the contour of his face. He said, "No Armstrong ever had that kind of music in him." Then, creakily, he was on his feet and fingering the lip of his bugle.

"For pity sake," mumbled Cal Royster, "it's just a kind of echo. . . ."

"Cal," said Spring, "if she comes real close to us, I'll blow the bugle for her."

Benjy didn't know why she should have been up again, loping through that timber. It was her voice, of course—no other dog had ever lived with such a melody hidden in its throat. He ventured to suppose that Bugle Ann had loved Spring Davis, much as a woman might have loved him, but it was a cruel and selfish devotion which would rob them all of their sanity, and never let them live in the same world with other men again.

He was repeating, again and again, "Pa! Pa—set down—set down—" and that was the same plea he had made in the bedroom.

Old Spring laughed at them all, and he seemed to tower against the sky. "Are you plumb certain that was her collar, Benjy? . . . I reckon nobody but God seen her bones hop up out of the orchard to-night."

He ceased speaking, then, because the
dog's howling was closer and more distinct,
as if the trail had swung toward the Hollow;
even now the fox might be leaping the gorge
of Chilly Branch. But Bugle Ann had learned
the last trick of any fox that ever jumped.

Bake Royster was trying to stand up, but
for the moment his legs wouldn't support him.
He thought, "She won't need any help to-
night. Spring Davis is in the woods, and nat-
urally she knows it." When he was far off in
the penitentiary it had been kind of the
Boone dogs, the hounds buried and dust a
hundred years ago, to come out and hunt
with her and cast in enormous circles to locate
the scent ... big, gobbling shapes, they could
drag down the fastest deer in the hills. They
could make the black bears afraid of them,
and every catamount would slink along the
tree-tops when they went by.

In sudden relief, Bake wanted to laugh out
loud. He had hoped that she was a ghost, all

along, for that made the whole tale so much easier to understand.

"Sweet mouth," he heard old Davis saying, "the sweetest mouth that ever lived."

Cal groped for his friend's arm. "Now, Spring," he quavered, "you got to get holt of yourself."

Spring laughed.

That clear, baying voice rocketed against the cloudy ceiling, and came down to wash all around them.

"Get holt? Why, I bred the most beautiful tune ever played in these parts, and I ain't ashamed! Maybe you laughed when you seen me bring this bugle, but I reckoned it would come handy." He paused, grinning slyly, and nodding again as the round pealing broke loose anew.

Then, from blackest distance and seeming to rise behind the hound notes, sounded the yell of a bugle. It blew the same chords which

Springfield Davis had always blown for his dog.

The hound's cry ceased, quickly, and the woods seemed to hold out empty hands.

The men looked at one another, pale face reflecting pale face, and for the first time you could see Springfield's eyes. They were bright with bewilderment, and with rage.

Once more the *ta-da*, the shrill witchery and command of it. The strings of old Davis's neck stood out tight against his skin. "I never done it," he cried. "I never gave no one else leave to blow her in!"

"Where was it?" asked Bake, hoarsely.

"Up on Heaven Hump, or past," Benjy answered him. Then he started away through the timber like a runaway steer, with Bake after him.

8

SPRING AND Cal stumbled cruelly in the underbrush, until the younger men called to each other, remembering, and came back to help them. Only when they had worked their way across Chilly Branch and had crept to the summit beyond, did any one say a complete sentence. It was Spring who spoke.

"Put out your lights," he ordered. "I see another fire."

A faint ruddiness lived in the north and east, and they went toward it. Benjy grasped his father's arm, pulling him along. The old man moved like a wooden image, but he breathed steadily, and Benjy was certain he'd never drop dead in those woods, no matter who or what they found beside that fire.

Again the tree-toads buzzed; the crickets

sawed and chuckled, and betty-millers came to kiss the hunters' perspiring faces; these creatures could be merry and could exalt their whispers again, with all those mighty trumpet notes echoed beyond recall.

The woods thinned away. Here was a clearing, stockaded with lonely fence posts, where once Jacob Terry's sheep had lain down in a green pasture.

A black shape grew against the distant core of firelight.

"It's a woman," said Bake.

For a moment he weaved, dizzy, as in the dawn before Jacob Terry was killed.

Camden Terry sat beside the blaze. She was motionless, even as the dry sticks crackled under approaching feet; she must have been expecting this invasion, all along. A dog was with her. The dog bayed, briefly, and Springfield Davis whispered, ". . . World, and they that dwell therein," and his arm tried to twist out of Benjy's manacling grasp.

The girl looked up at them. Benjy thought that she was more beautiful than ever—more beautiful than that day in court, for the fire made red gilt of her hair. Her eyes held dignity and fearlessness, but undoubtedly she was waiting for some immense judgment.

Spring stepped up against the fire, and looked down at the hound which crouched within the curve of the girl's arm. "You blew them notes," were the first words he said, for he saw the bugle in Camden Terry's lap.

She said, "Yes. Twice. Yes, I did."

"That hound—." His throat went to pieces on the word. He seemed to build it up again. "What dog is that?"

"I raised her."

"But it's got—her voice."

"Yes, I know. I used to hear her."

He said, scornfully, "I tell you, God never made no two hound-voices alike. Same kind of mouth, and all. He never."

The girl looked up at him. "This— She

was hers. She's Bugle Ann's. She's by Proctor Pride out of Bugle Ann. There were four more, but only this one had the real bugle-mouth."

Springfield staggered. Benjy held him. "She never had no pups," said Spring, thickly.

Camden passed her hand over the little hound's ears, and the dog watched Spring Davis with soft, sad eyes. Her nostrils reached out for the smell of him. . . . Camden Terry stood up; the bugle rolled across the ground. Firelight made her blue dress seem purple, and it did kindly with her eyes, and for a moment Benjy couldn't breathe.

"Mr. Davis," the girl said, "my father never killed her."

Spring cried, "Aw, we know that! The boys found her skeleton over by Bachelor's, and they heard her voice in the woods, but I still say she never was bred to any dog."

"That night—" Camden's voice was very

low; her hands struggled together. "I drove out of the yard, just like I told in court. She was coming past the gate; I couldn't see her in time. I couldn't— It was an awful sharp turn.... I got out and picked her up. ... She wasn't dead, and even—hurt—she— She didn't seem to blame me. I was afraid there'd be trouble over it: Bugle Ann's being hurt."

Somewhere in the world beyond, Cal Royster was saying, "Car lights. They stopped for a minute. Then they went on. It was when I heard the yip."

"This hound never was hers," Spring Davis snarled. "Where in hell did it get her voice?"

"Wait, Pa," said Benjy.

The girl's hands separated; the fingers flattened stiffly together. "I took her along in the car. The rest of my folks didn't know I'd brought her; just Uncle Elnathan. I told them I had found a run-over dog, on the way,

and I hustled her out to Uncle's place....
After we heard what had happened, I didn't
dare tell the truth. It would have been worse
for you, if the jury knew Bugle Ann wasn't
really dead at all."

She gasped, "Oh. I hated Pa. He killed my
mother with pure meanness. It's the awfulest
thing in the world to have a father you've
got to hate."

Spring eyed her grimly, and told her to
go on.

"Well, it was Bugle Ann's shoulder and
leg.... She was kind of crippled, but I nursed
her to health. When she came in heat in February, I bred her to Proctor Pride. He was a
Spaulding hound; the only good one Uncle
had, any more. There were five pups. But this
was the one—like her."

Camden paused, and there were tears all
over her face, but this time it was Benjy who
asked her to go on.

"She waited till they were weaned. Then she left one night—there was a moon— She wasn't dried up yet, and she wasn't strong enough to run. But she did go away. We traced her fifteen miles, next day, and then lost her for good. Likely she was heading for home when she struck a fox, and you folks heard her. We never knew she was dead, for sure, but I always thought she'd been killed trying to get back home."

Spring exclaimed, "Benjy, I got to set," and his son eased him quickly to the ground. ... Cal Royster fumbled around. It took him a long while to find his flask, but at last he did find it.

Soon, Spring opened his eyes and nodded at the girl. "You see," he murmured, "they let me out of Jefferson City."

Her chin trembled. "I knew. That's how I come to be here tonight. I thought you'd maybe be out in the timber."

Benjy stared at her with fierce intensity. "*You* knew. How did you know? They don't talk those things around."

"Well," she told him, "I knew beforehand."

Benjy said, "It wasn't a parole. He was pardoned."

"Yes. The parole board. Sometimes they —kind of recommend. Folks write letters. And talk."

He had taken her hand—both of her hands. He came between her and the Roysters, and he seemed even to have forgotten his father. Camden said, rapidly: "Jacob Terry was my father. I'd like to forget that, but it counted for something when they come to considering and— All my folks weren't Terrys," she cried at him. "Half of them were Camdens, and Camdens mean something in this state, even yet. Some of them are in the legislature."

Bake Royster exploded, "My God! You done it, didn't you?"

She shook her head. "No. I couldn't of done it myself. I just—did what I could. They all knew what kind of a man my father was. And I told them about Mr. Davis."

Inch by inch, the hound had hitched forward to sniff around Spring Davis's feet. At first the old man twisted his legs away, but finally he lay still and watched the dog. "I'm all right, boy," he muttered to Benjy, and then he raised up on his elbow. His eyes took in the whole color and shape and hide of the hound; they studied her slenderness, her strong and well-arched coupling, the stifle built far out from her body.... The hound sneezed. She looked at old Davis with curiosity, and then stepped across his legs with tail waving politely, and smelled him from the other side.

"I reckon she could run," said Spring.

"I trained her to the horn. Same as— It seemed like the best thing to do." Camden looked at Benjy, and he nodded slowly, and his face came close to hers.

Spring asked, "What do you call her?"

"Little Lady."

The old man said, "Got a deeper tan, but it's spotted much the same." Stiffly, reluctantly, he put out his hand and touched the hound's muzzle. His eyes were still hard and dry, but he whispered, "Little Lady. You got quite a mouth, Little Lady."

Cal Royster was crying like his own grandchild, but more quietly. Bake took him away from the fire. "Come on, Pa," he grunted, "we got to get out of here. I think I hear the pack coming north again." Baker was certain in his heart that before the other hounds had ever come in, Spring Davis would have sent Little Lady out with Camden and Benjy, to see what she was made of. He prophesied to himself that she would run as long as any fox made tracks; she would be

a twenty-hour dog, given to mighty journey-
ings and chasings, but always she would come
back to those black-dark hills when the bugle
called her home.

THE END